GIRLS SURVIVE

Girls Survive is published by Stone Arch Books, an imprint of Capstone.
1710 Roe Crest Drive
North Mankato, Minnesota 56003
www.capstonepub.com

Library of Congress Cataloging-in-Publication Data
Names: Gilbert, Julie, 1976- author. | Forsyth, Matt, illustrator. Title: Daisy and the deadly flu : a 1918 influenza survival story / by Julie Gilbert ; illustrated by Matt Forsyth. Other titles: Girls survive. Description: North Mankato, Minnesota : Stone Arch Books, a Capstone imprint, 2020. | Series: Girls survive | Audience: Ages 8-12. | Summary: Fourteen-year-old Daisy Meyer is angry and frustrated with her world: her German American town, New Ulm, is under surveillance, her father's newspaper was forced to shut down for criticizing the United States' entry into World War I, her beloved older sister Elsie's fiancé is deployed to France, and she deeply resents her stepmother--but worse is coming, because this is October 1918, and influenza is about to descend on her home and family, and it is not certain who will survive. Identifiers: LCCN 2019048024 (print) | LCCN 2019048025 (ebook) | ISBN 9781496587121 (hardcover) | ISBN 9781496592156 (paperback) | ISBN 9781496587138 (adobe pdf) Subjects: LCSH: Influenza Epidemic, 1918-1919--Minnesota--New Ulm--Juvenile fiction. | German American families--Minnesota--New Ulm--Juvenile fiction. | Sisters--Juvenile fiction. | Stepmothers--Juvenile fiction. | Ethnic relations--Juvenile fiction. | New Ulm (Minn.)--History--20th century--Juvenile fiction. | CYAC: Influenza Epidemic, 1918-1919--Fiction. | German Americans--Fiction. | Family life--Minnesota--New Ulm--Fiction. | Sisters--Fiction. | Stepmothers--Fiction. | New Ulm (Minn.)--History--20th century--Fiction. | LCGFT: Historical fiction. Classification: LCC PZ7.1.G549 Dai 2020 (print) | LCC PZ7.1.G549 (ebook) | DDC 813.6 [Fic]--dc23 LC record available at https://lccn.loc.gov/2019048024 LC ebook record available at https://lccn.loc.gov/2019048025

Summary:
In 1918, fourteen-year-old Daisy's family has fallen on hard times. Her sister Elsie's fiancé was recently deployed to fight in World War I, and her father's newspaper was forced to shut down for criticizing the U.S. entrance into the war. When the Spanish flu arrives in her small town in Minnesota, Daisy tries to shield her loved ones from the devastating illness. As the influenza pandemic sweeps through the nation, can Daisy protect those closest to home?

Image Credits
Library of Congress: Prints and Photographs Division, 104, 106; Shutterstock: Everett Historical, 103, 109, kaokiemonkey, (geometric pattern) design element throughout, Spalnic, (paper) design element throughout; Sarah Byrnes, 112

Designers: Cynthia Della-Rovere and Charmaine Whitman
Cover Artist: Alessia Trunfio

# DAISY
## AND THE **DEADLY FLU**
### A 1918 Influenza Survival Story

by Julie Gilbert

illustrated by Matt Forsyth

STONE ARCH BOOKS
a capstone imprint

I had a little bird,

And its name was Enza.

I opened the window

And in-flew-enza.

—*Children's jump rope rhyme, 1918*

# CHAPTER ONE

"Hand me a thimble?" my older sister, Elsie,
asked, glancing up from her embroidery. The sun
falling through the window turned her hair gold.
She looked like the princess in the book I was
reading. At seventeen, Elsie was everything
I wanted to be. Gracious and elegant, beautiful
and kind. But the thimble was on the other side of
the room, and I didn't want to get up.

I raised my book. "I just got to the good part."

"The kiss?" Elsie asked.

I wrinkled my face. "Ugh. No. The sword fight."

Elsie smiled and went back to her sewing.

A few minutes later, Elsie piped up. "Daisy, you have dirt on your face."

"What? Oh," I said, standing to peek in the mirror over the dresser. As usual, my face was smudged, and my hair was escaping its thick braids.

"Now that you're on your feet, can you get me that thimble?" she asked.

"Fine." I laughed, reaching for the thimble. There was nothing I wouldn't do for my older sister.

"Did you finish your essay about the Sedition Act?" Elsie asked.

"Yes," I said, my voice flat. The Sedition Act was a recent law that said people who criticized the government could be thrown in jail. In my essay, I wrote about how the law made me angry. I argued that newspapers should take a stand against it. If we didn't have free speech, what did we have?

"And?"

I shook my head. "It was a stupid plan. Papa's not going to reopen his newspaper just because of an essay I wrote."

My eyes slid to the desk drawer where I had shoved the pages after Papa handed them back to me a few days ago.

"Sorry, little flower, but I won't start up the newspaper," he had said. "The country is at war. It's too dangerous to print anything that doesn't support the war effort. Better not to print anything at all."

Papa had reason to be afraid. A little more than a year ago, someone had broken into Papa's newspaper, *The New Ulm Dispatch,* and destroyed the printing press. It was the summer of 1917, a few months after the United States had declared war on Germany. Papa had published several editorials protesting the war.

Most of us in town were German Americans. Many of us had cousins, uncles, and grandparents who still lived in Germany. If we went to war, we would be fighting against our friends and families.

We never found out who destroyed the press, but it scared Papa. I begged him to fix the press. I loved the newspaper. I wanted to be a reporter someday. Papa refused. He was terrified that he would be charged with unpatriotic behavior.

"Even if he wanted to reopen the paper, he couldn't afford to repair the printing press," Elsie said. "He's going to let us starve."

Elsie was angry we were running out of money to buy food. My stomach rumbled. I guess I was angry about that too.

I fingered a rip in my sleeve. "My cuff is torn," I said.

"Leave it in my basket tonight," Elsie said. "Do you want me to let out the hem too?"

"Sure," I said. "This has to last the winter. The She Monster said she wouldn't buy us new clothes until spring."

"Don't call her that," Elsie said mildly.

"I'll call her whatever I want," I protested. It was no secret I didn't like my stepmother. Bertha had nursed my mother through her final battle with tuberculosis seven years ago. Then she married my father six months after the funeral.

Bertha spent the first year of marriage rearranging the furniture and reading issues of *House Beautiful*. She ignored me completely. Then she had Joseph and spent all her time with the baby. I loved my little brother, but didn't Bertha even care about me?

"Read me the newspaper?" Elsie asked. "The last letter I had from Otto was two days ago."

Elsie's words were light, but her expression was serious. Her fiancé, Otto, had been drafted and was waiting to be shipped overseas to Europe. Right now he was training at Camp Dix in New Jersey. I knew Elsie was worried about him.

I grabbed the newspaper from the dresser. My eyes flew over the German script, skimming news about recent fighting in Belgium. There was also an update on the horrible fires that had swept through northern Minnesota two weeks ago. I gasped as my eyes fell on a headline.

"What is it?" Elsie asked.

"Influenza," I said. "There are more cases in the county. A few deaths. It's getting closer." Suddenly my torn cuff didn't seem so important.

Elsie and I had been tracking the progress of the Spanish flu, as it was called in the papers, for months. The flu was first reported at Fort Riley in Kansas last March when several hundred soldiers got sick. Everyone thought it had died out over the summer, but then it returned with a vengeance in

the fall. It hit the big cities first. Boston. New York. Philadelphia. Thousands of people died. And three weeks ago, the flu had reached Minnesota.

Elsie's eyes held mine. "It will be fine," she said. "We're fine. The city council closed all the schools and churches ten days ago. Even the bowling alley closed. We're safe here. No one comes or goes except for the postman and the milkman. We'll be fine."

"But you remember Hannah's letter," I began, panic rising in my throat. Elsie crossed herself quickly. The note from our cousin in Philadelphia had arrived two weeks ago. She wrote about how the flu had torn through their family, their neighborhood, and the entire city. Hannah's mother, our aunt Sofia, and Hannah's baby brother had both died. I still cried at Hannah's description of watching her mother struggle for breath at the end.

"That's different," Elsie said. "Hannah lives in

a city with a million other people. We live in the middle of a wheat field. The flu is a city problem. It can't touch us here."

I wanted to believe Elsie. I did. "But it's becoming a country problem," I said, nodding at the paper.

Elsie gave me a bleak look.

"Girls! I need you downstairs now!" our stepmother shouted. I sighed, and even Elsie rolled her eyes.

"Better go see what the She Monster wants," I said. I knew it was a childish nickname, but I felt grimly satisfied whenever I used it.

Elsie didn't bother to correct me.

As I passed by the window, something caught my eye. A rock stood next to a stump in the backyard. It was an ordinary-looking rock, the size of a small cat. It usually stood near the carriage house. Today it had been moved. It meant that my friend Daniel, who lived on the next farm, needed to see me. We had set up this signal years ago when we were little.

I'd go after dinner to see Daniel, I decided. Technically I was supposed to stay at home, because of the flu. But I told myself I just wouldn't hug Daniel or anything.

I flushed, thinking about hugging a boy. Then I shoved the idea out of my head and followed Elsie down the hall.

When we got downstairs, a small figure in blue barreled into us.

"I missed you! Come play with me!" our brother demanded. His small head barely reached my rib cage. Elsie grabbed him and swung him into her arms.

"We don't have time to play before dinner . . . but we do have time for tickling!" Elsie exclaimed, making Joseph scream with delight.

"Would you please be quiet!" Bertha demanded, appearing from the kitchen. The shapeless apron she wore was dusted in flour.

"Sorry, Mama," Joseph said. He grabbed his jacks and started to play happily in a corner of the dining room.

"Girls, I need you to set the table," Bertha said. "And one of you needs to watch Joseph. And someone has to stir the stew. I don't know how Agatha did it all before she left us."

"Agatha didn't leave us. You let her go because you couldn't pay her," I said.

Bertha looked like I had slapped her. I felt a stab of guilt. I felt even worse when Elsie stepped on my foot.

"Well, it smells wonderful, Bertha," my sister said. "Let me just head into the kitchen and see about the stew. Daisy will be happy to set the table." Elsie gave me a stern look. I tried not to roll my eyes.

"Here," Bertha said, pulling a stack of plates from the buffet. She turned to hand them to me. Suddenly a look of horror crossed her face. The plates fell from her hands, landing on the floor with a tremendous crash.

As Bertha screamed, I turned to see my little brother on the floor and turning blue.

# CHAPTER TWO

Thursday, October 24, 1918, 5:15 p.m.
The Meyer Home
New Ulm, Minnesota

"Joseph? Joseph!" Bertha screamed. She ran toward her son, bits of ceramic grinding into the rug beneath her boots.

"What was that noise?" Elsie asked, appearing in the doorway. She gasped as soon as she caught sight of Joseph. "Here," she said, shoving a dirty spoon at me.

I couldn't move. The spoon fell to the ground, spattering stew on the floorboards. I stared at Joseph, frozen in place. I couldn't breathe through my fear. Was it the flu? Was my little brother going to die? I'd read about cases where a person was fine at breakfast and dead by dinner.

Joseph coughed, and I was immediately transported back in time. I was standing outside my mother's room. Huge coughs shook her body. Her pale face turned toward the door. She asked me for water. And I couldn't move.

Just like now.

Bertha turned Joseph over her knee. Elsie gave him three smacks on his back. For a moment, nothing happened. In the awful silence, I heard Bertha sob.

Then Joseph coughed. He flinched as a small object popped out of his mouth.

Elsie gave a cry of joy as Joseph sat up and squinted at her.

"Ow, why did you hit me so hard?" Joseph asked, his voice raspy. He looked dazed.

"My baby!" Bertha cried, gathering Joseph in her arms. Tears streamed down her face.

"Mama, stop," Joseph protested, trying to squirm out of his mother's embrace. "Too many kisses!"

Bertha and Elsie both laughed, and Bertha laid her hand on Else's shoulder.

"You saved him," Bertha said.

"It was nothing," Elsie said, kissing Joseph's forehead. "Listen, little brother. No more putting strange things in your mouth, got it?"

"Got it," he said, flashing a huge grin. "Can I have some pie?" Elsie had made pie from apples from our trees. It was one of the few treats we still had.

"In a minute, sweetheart," Bertha said, patting Joseph all over as if she were afraid he'd broken a bone. Her face was a mixture of fear and relief.

My arms and legs trembled. I wanted to sit down, but I was afraid I would collapse if I tried to take a step. I should have gone to Joseph the instant I saw him turn blue. But all I could do was stand in the doorway, covered in bits of stew. I'd failed Joseph just like I had failed my mother.

"Daisy? You okay?" Elsie asked.

"I . . . um . . . I'm fine," I said, bending to pick up the spoon. My hands were still trembling. I knew I could tell Elsie why I was upset, but I didn't want Bertha to know. I'd wait until bedtime to talk to my sister. "I'll get a dustpan for the plates."

Bertha glanced at me. "Those plates were your mother's."

"Yes," I said. I waited to see if she was going to apologize, but she didn't.

"Mama, can I have some pie?" Joseph asked again.

"Sit at the table, and I'll get you a nice big piece," Bertha said. She was about to brush past me on her way to the kitchen when she stopped in front of the sideboard. She toed something with the tip of her boot. "Is this what you choked on?" Bertha asked. She bent to pick up the object and held it between her fingers.

"Yes," Joseph answered. "It was on the table. I thought it was gum."

I recognized it immediately. It was an eraser. One of my erasers.

She turned toward me, fury in her face. "What have I told you about leaving your writing things lying about?" she demanded.

"I didn't leave the eraser lying around!" I protested.

"He found it in this room," Bertha replied. "Which means you left it lying around. This is all your fault. He could have died!"

"It's not my fault! No one forced him to put it in his mouth."

"I don't want to hear it!" Bertha yelled. Her

voice rang in my ears. I had no idea she could be so loud. "My son almost died, and it *is* your fault."

The dam inside me broke. "I bet you broke Mother's plates on purpose!" I shouted, my braids flying around my shoulders. A part of me knew I wasn't making any sense, but I couldn't stop myself. "You're jealous of my mother's memory. You're a terrible woman!"

Bertha looked like she wanted to slap me. I gritted my teeth and glared at her.

"Daisy, stop it now," Elsie said.

I heard sobbing and realized that Joseph was crying.

"What's going on here? Elsie, Daisy, what is the meaning of this?"

I turned slowly to face my father. I wasn't tall for my age, but my father was a small man. We were almost the same height. Today, I hated having to look him in the eye.

"I . . . Joseph . . . ," I sputtered.

Bertha swept past me. "Your daughter almost killed our son."

"That's not exactly what happened," Elsie said.

"What did happen?" Papa asked. His mustache quivered. His eyes looked confused as they flitted from face to face.

"Joseph got hold of one of Daisy's erasers, and he choked on it," Elsie explained. "We got the eraser out. As you can see, he's fine."

We all looked at Joseph, who was staring at us. His lower lip started to tremble again. "Papa?" he asked.

"You've scared the boy," my father said, sliding past us. He bent and patted Joseph on the head. "You doing okay, little man?"

Joseph nodded, and his face brightened. "Can you get me some pie?"

Papa stood and held out his hand. Joseph hopped down from his chair. "Let's go," Papa said.

The two of them went into the kitchen hand in hand.

A cold silence fell over the dining room. Bertha glared at me.

"Today has been impossible. I'm going to bed," she huffed. The prisms in the chandelier clinked softly as she stomped out of the room.

I couldn't meet Elsie's eyes. I swallowed hard against the lump in my throat.

Elsie put her hand on my arm. "Listen, are you okay? That was rough just now."

"I'm glad Joseph is fine," I said. I looked over her shoulder at the blue patterned wallpaper. I didn't want to see the expression in my sister's face.

"That's not what I meant," Elsie said. "I meant what you said to Bertha."

My shoulders slumped. "I was upset."

"We all were," Elsie said. "I just wish you could learn to control your temper."

Just like that, my anger flared again. "Joseph choking wasn't my fault!"

"No one said it was."

"Bertha did," I said, my arms swinging wildly.

"She shouldn't have yelled at you, but she was afraid, Daisy," Elsie said. "Maybe someday you'll understand."

"Elsie, something is burning!" Joseph called from the kitchen.

"That would be the stew," Elsie said, wiping her hands on her apron. She paused at the kitchen door. "Just try to understand, Daisy."

I waited until she had disappeared before I stuck out my tongue. "Maybe someday someone will understand *me*," I said, stomping my foot. The remaining china rattled in the sideboard. I knew I should clean up the smashed plates. Instead, I left the room and went to bed, feeling miserable.

# CHAPTER **THREE**

The next morning, I lay in bed, watching the light outside the window change from black to gray. Images from the night before floated through my mind. Joseph choking. Me freezing. Bertha yelling. I groaned and rolled onto my stomach. I knew I was forgetting something, but I couldn't remember what. Then it hit me. Daniel's signal rock. In all the drama last night, I had forgotten about my friend. It was the first time he had signaled me in a while. I hoped nothing was wrong.

I threw back the quilt. My feet hit the cold floorboards, and I cursed softly beneath my breath. I always forgot to leave my slippers near the bed.

I padded to the washstand and splashed cold water on my face. After I dressed in my warmest dress and thick wool socks, I glanced into the hallway.

Elsie's room was empty. My sister always got up early to take eggs to the neighbors. There were a few older couples near us, and Elsie liked to check on them. Since the ban on public gatherings, however, Elsie had started leaving the baskets at the gate and waving.

Joseph's door was cracked open. His covers were tossed aside, and he was sprawled on his back. I paused for a moment to watch his chest rise and fall in his sleep. The door to Papa and Bertha's room was still closed.

I stole down the stairs. I skipped over the

creaky second step from the bottom and made my way through the dining room and into the kitchen. Someone had cleaned up the broken plates. The kitchen was spotless too. I felt a stab of guilt knowing Elsie had taken care of everything.

"I'll be helpful today," I promised, my voice quiet in the room.

I pulled on a pair of sturdy boots and wrapped my shawl around my shoulders. I found a few stale biscuits in the larder, which I slipped into my pocket. Then I lifted the latch on the back door and went outside.

The yard was slowly coming to life in the chill air. Sheets fluttered on the line tied between two trees. I could hear our horse, Luna, nickering in the stable. The chickens clucked and strutted about. I scattered a few handfuls of corn near the chicken coop.

"Hush," I said, waving my hand at the bobbling

chickens. They didn't listen to me, of course. One of the Rhode Island Reds came over to peck my boot.

I skirted the coop, heading for the line of trees that marked the edge of the yard. Rex, our hound dog, lumbered over to me.

"I'll be back soon. Stay," I said. Rex cocked a floppy ear at me and wandered away.

I took one of the paths through the forest. Last week, the leaves had been brilliant, vivid reds and yellows. More than half had already fallen. Soon the trees would be bare and winter would arrive. We would spend our evenings huddled around the stove in the kitchen. I would read by the flickering light, and Bertha would glare at me over her knitting needles. It's how we had spent last winter. I wasn't looking forward to it.

My boots made a soft shushing sound as I walked through the ankle-deep layer of leaves.

It made the paths harder to follow, but that didn't bother me. These paths were as familiar as the back of my own hand. Daniel and I had made most of them. When we were younger, the narrow forest between our two houses had been our kingdom.

Now Daniel and I rarely used the paths. After his father abandoned the family three years ago, Daniel dropped out of school and took over the farm. It was hard work. He had to support his mother and four younger sisters. His oldest sister, Betsy, was a couple of years younger than me, and his youngest sister, Molly, was my brother's age. Daniel worked from sunup to sundown, and they still barely had enough to eat. A part of me couldn't understand why Daniel or his mother didn't just sell the farm.

"It's home," was all he said when I asked him about it last year. I had been for a walk in the woods and ran into him. "You do whatever you can to save it."

*What would I do to save something I loved?*
I wondered. I snorted. I already knew the answer. I
would write an essay and try to have a discussion.
But what happens when you can't make a
difference?

I paused in the middle of the path. A hollow ache
filled my chest. I would give anything to go back to
a time to when life was simple and happy. Before the
war. Before the newspaper got destroyed. Before my
father married Bertha. Before my mother died.

"But that would mean no Joseph," I mumbled
to myself. Only a squirrel heard me, glaring at
me with beady eyes before scampering back into
trees. I decided not to think about these impossible
questions anymore.

I was breathing hard by the time I reached the
clearing behind Daniel's house. I barely noticed
when the shadows shifted and Daniel emerged from
the trees.

"Oh, you scared me," I said, pressing a hand to my heart. "I thought I'd have to leave a signal for you." Usually, Daniel left a red handkerchief in the crook of a tree whenever he signaled me. I would tie the handkerchief to a branch, which he could see from his farm. Then he'd know I was waiting for him.

"I'm sorry I didn't get here last night," I said, crossing the clearing.

"Stay back," Daniel said, holding up his hands. "Don't come any closer."

"Why?"

"Molly is sick." His dark eyes looked gravely into mine. Then he said more words, and the world shifted. "It's the Spanish flu."

I felt my knees buckle. "Is she going to be okay?" I asked. I could have kicked myself for saying it. What a stupid question. I had read the papers. I could recite my cousin's letter from

memory. The flu killed people at alarming rates. There was no guarantee Molly would be fine.

"It's not good," Daniel said, his voice flat. His shoulders slumped, and he sank onto a stump. "It came on so fast. We went to town two days ago to get supplies. Molly begged to go with me. I reminded her that everything had been shut down. Even the churches were closed. But we needed flour, and she promised to wait in the wagon. . . ." Daniel's voice trailed off. "I should never have taken her."

"You couldn't have known she would get sick just from a ride to town," I said.

"She followed me into the store," Daniel said grimly. "She wanted some penny candy. Then she woke up yesterday complaining of a headache. The next thing we knew, she was curled on the floor, shaking so hard she couldn't even get to her bed."

"How is she today?" I asked.

"It's awful," Daniel said. "She's coughing so hard I think she'll fall apart. Her skin is burning up from fever. I'm afraid."

"I am too," I whispered. I sank onto the stump, being careful to keep a wide space between us. Daniel had been exposed to the flu, and I didn't want to catch it.

I felt like I had been punched. I felt an overwhelming urge to race back to my house and bolt the door. Instead, I took a breath and reminded myself I had decided to be helpful. "What can I do?"

Daniel looked pained. I knew he hated asking for help. "Linens," he said. "We've gone through all the sheets we have. Molly keeps sweating so much. Maybe some blankets."

"Of course," I said. "I'll bring a bundle as soon as I can."

"Tie that to the branch," he said, pointing at the red handkerchief nestled in the tree.

"I will."

There was nothing more to say. Daniel gave me a wordless nod and slipped out of the clearing. I didn't stay to watch him go.

The branches tore at my clothes as I raced back to the house, desperate to get away from the flu. My braids whipped my face, and I was gasping for breath. It was still very dark outside. I stumbled through the trees, making my way to the house. I was almost home when a figure broke through the underbrush, making me scream.

# CHAPTER FOUR

---

Friday, October 25, 1918, 7:15 a.m.
The Meyer Home
New Ulm, Minnesota

---

Hands reached for me, settling on my shoulders.

"Daisy, Daisy it's me!"

I stopped struggling as soon as I recognized the voice.

"Papa. What are you doing out here?" I asked, trying to catch my breath.

"I was feeding the chickens, and I heard something rustling in the woods. You scared me, Daisy," he said.

I bit back a frightened laugh. "You scared *me!*"

Amusement glinted in Papa's eyes. For a brief

second, he was the vibrant man who loved to talk about books and ideas. Then he shook his head, and the amusement faded.

"Where have you been?" he asked.

"I was going for a walk."

"At daybreak?" Papa folded his arms across his chest. "Where were you, Daisy?"

"I went to see Daniel."

"Why?" he asked. "What were you discussing that couldn't wait until later?"

"His sister has the Spanish influenza."

Papa's hands fell from my shoulders. "Just like Sofia and the child," he whispered.

Sometimes I forgot that Hannah's mother was Papa's sister. We didn't see them very often since they lived in Philadelphia. But I still remember Aunt Sofia slipping me an extra potato dumpling the one time we visited them for Christmas, and laughing with Papa.

"What are we going to do?" I asked.

"Don't tell your stepmother. It will only make her worry more," he said, turning to head back to the house.

I nodded and followed.

We found Bertha in the kitchen, dumping oats into a pot. "We're almost out of oatmeal. I suppose we will have to make this stretch a few days," she said. "Close the door. It's cold."

I kept my face perfectly composed, but Bertha took one look at Papa and narrowed her eyes. "What is it?" she asked.

"It's nothing, Bertha," Papa said.

"Then why do you both look so frightened, Emil?" she asked.

Papa's hand rested heavily on my shoulder. I felt like if I moved, he would fall down.

"Emil. Tell me." I had never heard Bertha's voice sound so firm.

"The Schmidts have influenza," Papa said at last. "Daisy was just there."

Bertha turned so white that I thought she was going to faint. One hand clutched the back of a chair. She drew a deep breath and then she nodded. "Were you at the house?" she asked me.

"No, ma'am. I met Daniel in the clearing."

"Did you have any physical contact with him?" she asked. "Was he coughing? Did he breathe on you?"

"No, ma'am," I said.

Bertha fixed me with a level gaze. "That should be enough to keep the flu out of our house." She stirred the pot again. "Elsie is still out delivering eggs. Call Joseph," she said to me. "It's time for breakfast."

I could hear Bertha and Papa's low, murmured conversation in the kitchen as I left. I went to the bottom of the stairs. It took me two tries to clear my throat. "Breakfast!" I finally called, trying to keep the waver from my voice.

"Finally!" Joseph shrieked, streaking down the stairs. He wrapped his arms around me for a quick hug before dashing into the kitchen.

Breakfast was silent. I poked at my food, while Bertha stared at the ceiling. Joseph started talking about how he was going to play with the neighbor kids.

"You'll stay at the farm today," Bertha said, interrupting him. "No friends."

"What? Why?" Joseph asked.

"Because I said so."

Bertha's tone was enough to quiet my brother, although his lower lip started to tremble. I gave his arm a squeeze and slipped him part of my oatmeal, which he ate happily.

I heard a clattering sound over the clink of our spoons against the bowls. I raised my head. The sound was coming from outside. The others noticed it too.

"Uncle Peter!" Joseph shouted. Bertha's brother was the town doctor. There were a few other people who had automobiles in town, but the doctor was the only one who came to visit us. Joseph hopped off his chair and raced toward the front of the house.

"What on earth could my brother want?" Bertha muttered, looking worried.

"He's the doctor," Papa reminded her. A muscle in his jaw clenched. "He's probably here to tell us about the flu. I just hope he doesn't want your help."

Bertha gave my father a sharp glance as we all left the table. I wondered what it meant.

The morning was still cool when we stepped onto the porch. A dusty Model T puttered past the lilac bushes that lined the drive. Peter Bender was a tall, lanky man. I didn't know him well, but he was always nice to us. Dr. Bender shifted the brake lever and unfolded himself from the automobile.

"I wish I was coming with better news," he said. "But influenza has reached town."

"We know," Papa said.

"You do?" the doctor replied. "How? Are any of you sick?"

"No," Papa shook his head. "But we heard it was at the Schmidt farm."

Dr. Bender nodded, his frown making his mustache droop. "Did any of you come into contact with any of the Schmidts?"

"I saw Daniel this morning," I said. "In the woods. But we didn't touch."

"Did he spit on the ground or cough near you?" Dr. Bender asked.

"No," I said.

"Good," he said. "Keep it that way. All of you." He pulled something from the front seat of the

Model T. "Stay home. Don't associate with anyone who has symptoms. Wear these masks if you leave the house." He handed a stack of white cloth to Bertha.

"How are you holding up?" Bertha asked.

"Not well," he said. "My nurse is sick, and I'm not able to make calls to the rural areas to check on patients."

Bertha drew in a breath. "Then I'll come with you," she said.

"No," Papa and Dr. Bender said at the same time.

Bertha glared at both of them. "I'm a trained nurse."

"What about Joseph? And us?" Papa asked.

My stepmother's hand trembled slightly on Joseph's shoulder. "I wouldn't do this unless it was absolutely necessary," she said. "I've read the papers. I know how bad it is."

"Bertha—" Papa started.

But Bertha interrupted him. "I'll wear the mask.
I'll wash my hands so much the skin will turn red.
And I'll disinfect every surface."

"But we need you," Papa said.

"I know that," Bertha said. "I'm not making this
decision lightly. I won't come back until I'm sure
I'm not sick."

"Bertie, it's too dangerous," Dr. Bender said.

"It's too dangerous for me but not for you?"
she asked. "I wanted to be a nurse all my life.
It was hard work, but I did it. This is my job. And
I'm going to do it."

She bent down before Joseph. "You stay here
and mind your sisters." Her eyes flittered to me, and
I nodded.

"I didn't come here to ask you," Dr. Bender said.

"I know," said Bertha.

"But thank you," he said.

Bertha brushed a quick kiss on Joseph's forehead. "Take care of yourself, little man. Mama will be home soon," she said.

Papa stayed on the porch as Bertha walked down the steps and got into the automobile.

The flu found a way, no matter how careful you were. As I watched Bertha and her brother drive away, I couldn't shake the feeling that I might never see her again.

# CHAPTER FIVE

Friday, October 25, 1918, 8:00 a.m.
The Schmidt Farm
New Ulm, Minnesota

When we went back to the house, I wandered from room to room. I wasn't sure what to do. I was too anxious to read or write. Elsie wouldn't be back for another half hour at least. What would I tell her about our stepmother? Bertha's bravery impressed me.

A weird feeling gnawed my stomach. With surprise, I realized it was worry. Was I actually worried about my stepmother?

I fingered the pile of masks Papa had set on the hall table. There was a tie on each corner to

fasten around the back of the head. The fabric was
so thin.

*Fabric. Daniel.*

It came back to me in a rush. I had promised
Daniel I would bring him fresh sheets. After shoving
a few masks into my pocket, I darted into the
backyard. Yesterday's laundry still hung on the line.
The sheets smelled like warm hay and lavender. I
gathered several and brought them into the kitchen.
I took a few jars of preserves from the larder and
wrapped them carefully in the sheets. I shoved the
sheets into a basket, which I slung over my arm.

I didn't bother telling Papa I was going. He'd
tell me to stay in the house, but I needed to help my
friend. I wouldn't get too close. But I would try to
help.

I retraced my steps from this morning. When
I reached the clearing, I glanced at the path leading
back to my house. I could be home before Papa

even knew I left. I thought of my stepmother and her decision to help the sick. I wouldn't put myself in danger, but I wanted to know how Daniel's family was.

After a few minutes, I walked down the hill to Daniel's house. I could drop off the materials and be home soon. I would do what Elsie did when she delivered eggs. I'd leave the basket at the gate and call to him. I wouldn't get close.

Daniel's house squatted in a shallow valley. A stream ran through the yard, dividing the farmyard from the fields, which were dotted with the stubbles of wheat stalks. At least Daniel had managed to get the harvest in this year. Rusty farm equipment littered the yard, peeking out of long grasses. Paint was peeling, and the roof needed to be replaced. The entire farm looked abandoned except for a thin trickle of smoke coming from the chimney.

A rangy dog started barking at my approach.

Daniel appeared in the doorway, shushing the dog. I paused at the gate.

"What are you doing here?" he gasped, stepping onto the sagging porch. "You should have just left the sheets near the stump."

"I wanted to see if you needed more help," I said. "How's Molly?"

Daniel's face looked worn, and he shook his head. "Her fever's worse. She was better for a few hours, but now she's burning up again. I'm scared, Daisy," he said, his voice breaking. "Lily and Dottie are sick now too. Plus Mama."

"Your mother is sick? And all your sisters?"

"All except Betsy," he said, drawing a ragged breath. "Just put the bundle on the ground. Then go."

My hands shook as I set the basket on the ground. What if Daniel lost his entire family? What if the flu kept coming and every single person in New Ulm was wiped out? What if this was the end of everything?

I knew people recovered from the flu. I knew it wouldn't kill all of us. But what if it just kept getting worse?

Suddenly a scream came from inside the house. Daniel raced inside. Without thinking, I followed fast on his heels, then immediately wondered if I should've stayed put.

I paused on the porch and fumbled for one of the masks I had shoved in my pocket. My fingers were trembling as I tied it around the back of my head. I remembered what Bertha said about washing her hands and disinfectant. I would do what I could to protect myself. But Daniel's entire family was sick. I needed to help.

I went through the door.

As soon as I got inside, I wished I had stayed in the yard. The stench of unwashed bodies and sickness made my eyes water. Two mattresses had been dragged in front of the stove. Lily and Dottie lay on one. Daniel's mother lay on the other, curled around a small form I recognized as Molly. I felt my heart clench.

Betsy stood with her back pressed against the wall, staring at their mother.

"Betsy, why did you scream?" Daniel demanded.

"I thought Mother was gone," she whispered.

Daniel dropped to his knees next to his mother's mattress. He pressed his hand to her forehead and then laid his ear against her chest.

"She's not gone," he said, leaning back. "Not yet."

He dipped a rag in a bucket near the stove and laid a damp cloth across his mother's forehead. I could hear him whispering to her in German, but I was too far away to make out the words. His mother shivered, and Daniel drew a blanket over her shoulders.

I looked around the room, trying to think of something I could do to help. A layer of dust covered the table, and two full chamber pots stood near the

door. I tried not to gag. The fabric from my mask clung to mouth.

A few minutes ago, I had been in the clearing, filling my lungs with fresh, clean air. I could go back there. I could leave. I could turn and walk out of the house and never look back. I could leave Daniel to deal with the situation on his own.

I hated myself for those thoughts. I knew a good friend would stay and let Daniel get some rest. A good friend would empty the chamber pots and clean the table and disinfect every surface.

One of the girls on the other mattress began to cough. I heard whispers of my mother's cough. I froze. I was a fool for coming here. The flu was bigger than me. I couldn't stop it. People would die no matter what I did, just like my mother. I was foolish to think I could make a difference.

Just then, blood began pouring from Mrs. Schmidt's nose.

# CHAPTER **SIX**

Daniel moved quickly, scooping Molly from the mattress and moving her next to her sisters. He caught sight of me.

"You shouldn't be here," he said.

"I know," I whispered.

I bent to check on Molly. She was so frail that I could see every bone. She coughed, and I jumped backward.

Time slowed. I was aware of Daniel bent over his mother, trying to stop the bleeding. I could hear my pulse whooshing through my ear. I felt lightheaded. Spots danced in front of my eyes. I felt like I was going to vomit.

I bolted out the front door, paying no attention to where I was going. All I knew was that I had to get away from Daniel's farm. The smell lingered in my nose. I couldn't erase the image of Daniel's mother bleeding from her nose or Molly's frail body.

I had done nothing except expose myself to the Spanish flu. Now I couldn't even go home for fear of infecting my family.

I was on the main road about a mile from my house. The skeleton arms of trees arched overhead, and the sky was so gray and heavy I thought it might fall on me.

I put my head down and kept running. I was heading in the direction of the river. A part of me had the crazy idea to jump into the water. It didn't matter that the river would be cold. Maybe I could wash myself clean.

I stopped when I realized someone was shouting my name. When I whirled around, I came face-to-face with Clara Voss, who lived on a big farm on the ridge and was a year behind me in school. Clara was wearing a mask over her face, just like me.

"Stay away!" I shouted. "I might have the flu."

Clara turned so pale that the freckles scattered across her cheeks looked like red confetti. "Why are you outside, Daisy?" she asked. "You should be home in bed!"

"I was just coming back from Daniel Schmidt's farm," I explained. "They're all sick."

Clara's dark hair slid across her shoulders as she shook her head. "It's everywhere, isn't it?" Her voice sounded lost.

I took a closer look at her. "Clara, are you okay?"

"My mother is sick," she said, sighing. "Came down with it two days ago. She keeps asking for milk, but the milkman fell ill and didn't deliver today. I was going to see if any of the neighbors had a fresh pail they would be willing to share."

Tears began rolling down Clara's face. A sob tore from my throat. I knew what it was like to have a dying mother. I wrapped my arms around her. We had both been exposed to the flu, so it didn't matter if we touched.

"I'm so scared," Clara said, her voice muffled by my shoulder.

"I know. Me too."

"Did you know the Herberts both died?" she asked.

A chill went down my spine. "The mother and daughter who live on the other side of the ravine?" I asked.

Clara nodded. "The postman told me. I went

past their house this morning, and there's black crepe on the doors."

It was customary to drape heavy fabric over the doors of a house whenever there was a death. An image of every single house in New Ulm covered in crepe flashed through my mind.

For weeks, I'd been reading about the flu in far-off areas. But now influenza was in New Ulm, and there was no escaping it. It wasn't a war that was being fought overseas, in countries I might never see. It was a war we were fighting in our very own homes. The place that was supposed to be the safest was actually the deadliest.

"Did the postman say who else is sick?" I asked.

"The Becker girls all have influenza," Clara said. "And I heard that Lonnie Sumners took a turn for the worse last night."

I gulped. Lonnie was one of my classmates.

"Someone said it was worse in the country,"

she continued. "They didn't hear about the ban on public meetings until it was too late."

Clara was trembling, and there was a sheen of sweat on her face. I pressed my hand to her head. She was burning up. I didn't know if it was the flu or if she was simply exhausted.

"Clara, you need to get home," I said as gently as I could. "Do you want me to walk you?"

"You're right. I don't feel so well," Clara said, looking dazed as I took her elbow. Her house was a mile down the road. We didn't talk the rest of the way.

When we got to her house, Clara squeezed my hand. "I'll go the rest of the way myself."

I watched until Clara made her way up the stairs, her steps wobbling slightly. I said a prayer that Clara got well. Then I watched as the house swallowed her up.

There was nothing left to do but to return to my

family. It was over a mile, and my feet dragged the entire way.

When I got home, I stood in the yard. I couldn't go inside. I had been exposed to the flu. The newspaper had printed guidelines from the State Health Board. We were supposed to disinfect contaminated surfaces with a solution of carbolic acid. Maybe Papa could set up a tub in the backyard and I could jump in.

My knees buckled and I sank to the ground, drawing my knees to my chest. I felt dirty and diseased. Huge sobs tore from my chest. Rex ambled over to nudge my hand. I buried my face in his neck. At least the dog could still touch me.

"Why are you crying?" a small voice called from the porch.

I looked up and saw Joseph watching me from the door, his thumb in his mouth. "Stay where you are," I said, stumbling to my feet. "I've been exposed to the flu." Then I frowned, confused. Joseph only sucked his thumb when something was upsetting him.

"So you're sick too?" Joseph asked.

"Wait, what did you mean that I'm sick *too*?" I asked. "Who else is sick?"

Joseph took his thumb out of his mouth and said one awful word: "Elsie."

# CHAPTER SEVEN

Friday, October 25, 1918, 9:15 a.m.
The Meyer Home
New Ulm, Minnesota

"What did you say?" I asked.

Joseph watched me with wary eyes. "Elsie is sick."

His words felt like a thousand arrows slamming into my stomach.

"No," I said slowly. I shook my head. "She can't be sick."

"But Papa—"

"I said she's not sick, Joseph!"

Tears welled up in my brother's eyes and spilled down his face.

"Go get Papa," I said, trying to keep my voice level. "Tell him I'm in the yard."

Joseph slipped through the door. A moment later, my father stumbled onto the porch. He clutched the railing as if it was the only thing holding him upright. He didn't look at me.

"Papa, what did Joseph mean about Elsie?" I asked.

My father shook his head.

"Papa," I repeated, my voice sharp.

Finally he looked up at me, his face drawn. "She came back from delivering the eggs and complained that the light was hurting her eyes. When Joseph hugged her, she collapsed on the porch."

Horror gripped my chest. "She touched Joseph."

Tears started streaming down Papa's face. "Yes. He's been exposed and so have I. We're so lucky that you are okay, Daisy. My little flower will be fine."

My hands shook when he called me that. "I was
exposed about an hour ago. At Daniel's house."

Papa's face turned gray. I untied my mask and
shoved the balled-up fabric into my coat pocket.
I crossed the yard slowly and walked up the porch
steps toward my father. I laid a hand on his shoulder.
He reached up and gripped my hand. An odd feeling
of relief flowed through me. If flu was already
inside the house, I didn't need to exile myself from
my family.

"We should go check on Elsie," I said at last.

The stench of hot vinegar hit me as soon as we
stepped into the kitchen. "What is that smell?"
I asked.

"Medicine," Papa said, hurrying to the huge pot
bubbling on the stove.

I glanced at Joseph, who shrugged. "My job was
honey," he said.

"What?" I asked.

"I heard about it from the Herberts at church a few weeks ago," Papa said. "You boil vinegar with onions and herbs. Joseph added the honey to make it taste better."

"But the Herberts both died," I blurted. "I heard about it on my way back home."

The ladle fell from Papa's fingers.

"I'm sorry," I said.

"You should go check on your sister," Papa said. He handed me a glass of water. "Maybe this will help."

I didn't bother taking off my boots as I climbed the stairs and walked down the hall to my sister's room.

"Elsie? Elsie, it's Daisy. Can you hear me?"

The soft light that crept around the edge of the drapes made the room seem dreamlike. Elsie lay still on her feather bed. She wore a long white nightgown and was covered by a patchwork quilt.

She looked like a princess asleep in a fairy tale.

It was almost peaceful.

Then I took a step closer to Elsie's bed, and the spell was broken. I could hear the rasp of my sister's breathing. As I set the water glass on the bedside table, I caught a whiff of Elsie's stale breath. Sweat had dried on her forehead and matted her lovely hair. Her legs twitched beneath the covers. I reached down and pulled the quilt over her shoulders, but she shuddered and threw it off.

"Elsie, I'm here," I said, but she never opened her eyes. I brushed strands of hair from her forehead. Her skin was burning up.

"Elsie, please be okay," I said, my voice breaking. "Please."

I sat on a chair beside the bed and reached for the glass.

"Here, I have something for you," I said. I moved so I could slip an arm around Elsie's shoulders. I braced my feet against the floor and lifted her to a sitting position. Her head lolled against my shoulder. Her eyes remained closed.

"Elsie, I have some water for you." I realized I couldn't pick up the glass at this angle.

I swore softly. Tears pricked my eyes as I laid Elsie down. She flopped onto the bed, moaning slightly.

"Daisy . . . ," she said, her eyelids flickering.

"Yes, it's me!" I cried. My sister recognized me, and I felt like I could cry with joy.

"Otto, you're here," Elsie continued. "I missed you."

I glanced around the room, half-expecting Otto to walk through the door with his bright brown eyes and huge smile. The room was empty.

"Elsie, Otto's not here," I said.

My sister groaned once, and then she was silent. I sat and watched her chest rise and fall unevenly.

"You're going to be okay," I whispered. "I promise."

Just then, the doorbell rang. My breath caught in my throat. Between the war and the instructions to stay at home, it could only be bad news.

When I got to the top of the stairs, I froze. Papa was standing in the open doorway, holding a fragile slip of paper. His fingers trembled. Over his shoulder, I could see the retreating form of the telegram delivery man. I felt dizzy. Telegrams during the war only meant bad news.

I must have made some kind of sound, because Papa looked up at me. His face was pained.

"Daisy," he said seriously. "It's Otto. He's dead."

# CHAPTER EIGHT

"No," I said to my father, keeping my voice low so Elsie didn't hear. "Otto can't be dead. It must be a mistake. They didn't ship him overseas yet. He's fine."

"There's no mistake," Papa said, waving the telegram at me. "Otto is gone."

"How?" Tears rolled down my face. Every time he visited, Otto brought me books. He and Elsie let me tag along with them on their walks, and Otto always asked me about what I'd read. I thought we'd have years to do this.

"He had influenza," Papa said. He sighed, sagging against the banister. "That poor boy. He had so much promise. He wanted to be a teacher." Papa's eyes found mine. "Daisy, promise me you won't tell your sister."

"We're going to lie to her?" I was shocked. Papa raised us to never tell a lie.

"We'll tell her once she's better," Papa replied. "I'm afraid if she knew her fiancé was gone, she might give up."

With heavy feet, I went back to Elsie's room. My sister was restless, moaning slightly as she rocked back and forth against the pillow. She had kicked off her blankets, and her nightgown was tangled around her legs.

I looked around the room. What was I supposed to do? How was I supposed to help my sister? A surge of anxious energy pulsed through my veins. I grabbed a pile of towels and began folding and refolding them.

"No, this isn't helping," I muttered under my breath. I dropped the towels.

I dipped a soft towel in the water and laid it across my sister's face. She flinched at first, but then she stilled.

"It's going to be okay, Elsie," I whispered. "I'm here. I'll take care of you. You'll get better, and soon we'll be going on long walks through the fields and planning your wedding."

My voice cracked on the last word. There would be no wedding to plan.

"And then it will be Christmas and sledding parties and hot cocoa," I continued, trying to keep my voice strong. "We'll light all the candles on the tree and eat big slices of stollen." My mouth watered at the thought of the holiday bread stuffed with bits of marzipan and candied fruit. "Just wait. It will be the best Christmas ever."

Tears filled my eyes, but I gritted my jaw and

forced them back. Unwillingly, I pictured an empty chair at the holiday table, a sad Christmas tree with no presents. What if Elsie died? I couldn't stand the thought. Death had already taken my mother and Otto. I refused to let it take Elsie. I wiped my nose on my sleeve and realized I hadn't even taken off my coat.

"I'm going to stay right here until you're better," I said. "I promise."

I sat by the bed for hours, pressing a damp cloth to Elsie's forehead. She didn't wake from her restless sleep except to sneeze once or twice. Then she'd fall back on the pillow, unconscious. I talked about anything that popped into my mind, from school to the plot of a story I was writing for Joseph. I wanted Elsie to know she wasn't alone.

Toward midafternoon, Elsie started coughing. Her entire body shuddered and she bent in half, clutching her arms over her stomach. I thought she might break apart. I pressed a hand to her forehead. She was burning up. The flu was getting worse.

"Elsie? Have some water," I said, reaching for a glass. As I leaned toward my sister, the room went out of focus.

Just like that, I was seven again and standing in the hall, listening to my mother cough. I couldn't breathe. I couldn't move. I couldn't help Elsie, just as I couldn't help my mother all those years ago. Or how I couldn't help Joseph when he had choked or Molly as she suffered on the mattress.

Elsie's arm flailed, knocking the glass. Water spilled over both of us, jarring me from my memory.

I took a deep breath. I could do this. I could take care of my sister. I wasn't going to fail her. "Sorry about that, Elsie," I said, wiping water from her face with a towel. "I'll be more careful next time."

"Daisy?" she said. Elsie was looking at me with dazed eyes.

A huge grin spread across my face. "Yes, it's me. How are you feeling?"

Elsie frowned and shook her head. "I feel terrible. And I'm all wet."

"That was my fault," I said, still smiling. "Let's get you cleaned up."

Somehow I managed to get Elsie into a fresh nightgown. She was able to sit in a chair while I changed the sheets. By the time I got her back into bed, she was drifting to sleep.

"You'll see, it will all be fine," I said, pulling the covers up to her chin. I laid a hand on her forehead. "Your fever broke. See, you're going to be just fine."

I sat back in the chair I had pulled over to the side of the bed. Feelings of relief spread through me. I had nursed Elsie through the worst of it. She was going to be fine. We all were.

I must have dozed, because suddenly I was dreaming. I stood on the back porch, the rough sound of a handsaw in my ears. The trees in my forest had all been cut down. All that remained were jagged stumps. I was devastated. Tears streamed down my face as I ran toward the broken trees. The sound of the saw chased me, coming closer and closer until I woke with a start.

My heart was racing. I could still hear the sound of the saw. I jumped as I looked at the bed. The ragged sound was Elsie's breathing. My sister looked terrible. Her skin was gray and sweaty. She was surrounded by rags splattered with blood.

"Elsie?" I cried, reaching for my sister.

"Stay back, Daisy," someone said. I watched as a pair of strong, capable hands removed the rags.

I looked up into my stepmother's eyes. Bertha's face was covered by a mask.

"What are you doing here?" I asked. "What day is it?"

"It's still Friday. Your father sent a message

with the telegram operator. I came back as soon as I could."

"I had it under control," I protested, my temper flaring. The room spun slightly as I sat up. "I nursed her through the flu! Her fever broke, and she was fine until you came back."

An expression flitted through Bertha's eyes—one I had never seen before. It almost looked like compassion.

"Daisy, you did a remarkable job taking care of Elsie," Bertha said. "But she's not safe yet."

"She doesn't have a fever anymore," I protested.

"The influenza fever comes and goes. Hers is back," Bertha said.

"Oh," I replied.

"Daisy, I meant it. You did an amazing job taking care of Elsie," Bertha repeated.

"Is Joseph okay? And my dad?" I asked.

"So far neither of them are showing symptoms,"

she replied. "They are going to sleep in the hayloft tonight. Against my better judgment, but it keeps Joseph out of the way."

"Good," I said, nodding. My neck was stiff. In fact, my whole body was aching. I pressed a hand to my forehead, where a headache was starting. It must've been the way I'd slept in the chair. "What can I do to help?" The room spun for a moment.

"You can put a mask back on to start," Bertha said. "And then help me boil some water to disinfect these linens."

I knew something was wrong when I tried to stand up. Waves of dizziness washed over me, and my legs gave out. Pain shot through my head, along with a terrible realization.

"Daisy?" Bertha's voice was high as she reached for me.

"I think I'm sick," I said, right before I collapsed.

# CHAPTER NINE

Hands patted my hair and touched my face. I felt both cold and hot at once. I tried to open my eyes, but they were glued shut. I heard someone groaning and realized it was me.

"Hush, Daisy," a soft voice said. "You need to preserve your strength."

"Mama?" I cried.

The hands withdrew slightly.

"Don't go, Mama," I whispered. "I'm so scared."

"There's no reason to be scared," the voice said. "You are strong and brave. You will make it through this."

"So tired," I said.

"I know. Go to sleep now."

Someone pulled the blanket around my shoulders, and I fell into a fitful sleep. In my dreams, I ran through forest trails, hunted by monsters. Other times I opened my eyes and my room became the nightmare. The walls moved, and once the ceiling collapsed before jerking back into place.

Sometimes I coughed. Pain shot through my chest. I looked down and saw spatters of bright-red blood on a white towel. I realized someone was holding me.

"Mama?" I asked, fingering the worn fabric of her blouse.

"Get some sleep, Daisy," the voice said, laying me back on the pillow.

When I opened my eyes, it was dark. But then I blinked and suddenly it was light. Everything hurt. My throat felt like sandpaper.

"Water," I whispered.

A glass appeared at my mouth. When I tried to swallow, half the water ran down my front. Someone pressed a towel to my neck, stirring a memory. I had wiped my sister's face when she spilled water. I couldn't remember why or where.

"Elsie," I moaned. "Elsie, I'm coming to find you."

"Hush, dear," a voice said. It wasn't Elsie. I wanted to ask for Elsie, but the words got stuck in my throat. I drifted to sleep again, waking when it was light, but then suddenly it was dark again. My legs felt like someone had tied stones around them and thrown me into a lake. I tried to swim to the surface, but the deep water kept pulling me down.

"How is she?" someone asked. I realized it was my father.

"Not out of the worst of it yet," a voice replied.

It was Bertha. I twisted on the mattress, fever burning my skin.

"Do you need anything?" my father asked.

*I need you to pull me out of the lake*, I thought, but he wasn't talking to me.

"It's almost time for her next dose of aspirin," Bertha said. "And I'll need more linens within the hour. You're boiling the sheets, right?"

"Of course, dear."

"Good. And Joseph isn't showing any signs of sickness?"

"Not yet, thank heavens. I'll be back soon."

The door creaked closed. I tried to stay awake. The next time my father came through the door, I would push myself out of the lake.

But the next time I opened my eyes, the evening light was spilling across the floor. I took a breath. My chest hurt, but I didn't feel like I was going to cough. I still had a headache, but it no longer felt like my head was going to split in two. I stared at the ceiling, wondering if it would start moving again. When it stayed still, I lifted my head.

Bertha sat in a chair near my bed, her eyes closed. She was wearing an old dress, and her hair was pulled back in a long braid. Lines of worry marred her forehead. I had a sudden memory of Bertha sitting in a chair next to my mother's bed. I had run when my mother coughed. Bertha had been the one to get her water.

I shifted on the bed, and Bertha awoke. Her eyes were bloodshot, but she smiled when she saw me.

"How are you feeling?" she asked.

"Better," I said.

Bertha pressed her hand to my forehead. "The worst is over. You're going to recover."

"What day is it?" I asked.

"Monday."

"Oh," I said, and then I fell asleep again. When

I woke up, it was morning. Bertha was still at my side. She gave a soft smile when she saw I was awake. I felt much better.

"You took care of me," I whispered, even though it hurt to talk. "You stayed with me."

"Of course I did," she said, pressing a hand to my forehead. "You're my daughter."

"Stepdaughter," I corrected.

Bertha frowned. "I know I haven't been the mother I should have been to you, Daisy. But I do think of you as my daughter."

"Why did you marry Papa?" I blurted.

"Lots of reasons," Bertha said with a smile. "He was kind, and we had grown close after your mother's death. I liked the idea of having a family of my own." She smoothed the blankets around my shoulders. "Your father is a wonderful man, but he has no idea how to run a house or raise children."

I nibbled on my bottom lip, considering her words.

"And then after he shut down the press," she continued, "you needed me even more."

"He gave up," I said.

Bertha tilted her head, regarding me with curious eyes. "They would have thrown him in jail, Daisy. The Public Safety Commission made it perfectly clear they would have prosecuted him if he kept writing. They did it to other newspaper editors."

"Oh," I said. I hadn't known that.

Bertha's smile was tired. "Wartime is always terrible, especially if you look like the enemy. You've heard the rumors that the Germans are spreading the flu. And you remember what happened in Luverne."

I nodded. In August, a German American farmer in a nearby town had been kidnapped, tarred, and feathered by a group of men. All because they didn't think he was patriotic enough.

I coughed a little. Bertha poured me a glass of water and helped me drink.

"You should get some rest now, Daisy," she said.

There was something I should be asking, but I couldn't think what it was. "You didn't try to get to know me," I said instead. I guess the flu made me feel like telling the truth.

"I should have tried harder," Bertha admitted. "You spent most of the first summer outdoors anyway, playing with your friends and Elsie."

Elsie. That was it. She was sick.

"How is Elsie? Is she better?" I asked.

I caught the moment when Bertha's eyes changed, filling with worry.

"Tell me," I said. I thought about how Papa said not to tell Elsie about Otto. Were they keeping news of Elsie from me?

"She's not well," Bertha said at last. "My brother is with her now, but Daisy, there's not much he can do."

"No," I said. "No, she's going to be fine."

I fought my stepmother's hands as I lugged myself out of bed and stumbled down the hall.

"Elsie? Elsie!" I cried. I couldn't lose my sister.

The hall spun, and my legs buckled. I clutched the wall to keep from falling. Somehow I got to Elsie's room.

The door was open. My sister lay in a tangle of sheets, her face blue. My father clutched her hand. Dr. Bender pressed a finger to her throat. Bertha pushed herself into the room behind me.

I could see what was coming. I could see it in Bertha's face and my father's tears. I could hear it in Elsie's rasping lungs. I could see it, but I couldn't stop it. All I could do was cling to the doorway and watch in horror as my sister took her final breath.

# CHAPTER TEN

The grass over my mother's grave was thick and green, but the ground over my sister's was still bare.

My heart was similarly bare. It had been seven months since Elsie died. I missed her every single moment.

"The shrubs we planted won't bloom until next year, so I brought you some flowers from the yard," I said, arranging Mason jars around the base of the headstone. The scent of lilac blossoms filled my nose. "Bertha showed me how to sear the cut ends on the stove so they'll last longer."

My voice cracked slightly, and I wiped the tears that formed in the corner of my eyes. "School will be out soon," I continued. "I'll be watching Joseph in the mornings while Bertha helps her brother at the hospital."

I leaned against the headstone, feeling a slight chill creep into my spine. I curled my hands in the lush grass and watched a butterfly land on the drooping purple lilacs.

"Joseph kept us all together, you know," I said, glancing down the rows where my brother played among the stones. "At Christmas, he was the one who insisted we put up a tree. And of course, he demanded presents," I said with a smile. "But he reminded us that there was still light and love in our lives."

As if sensing I was talking about him, my brother lifted his head and waved. I waved back.

"I still can't believe you're gone," I whispered.

I barely remember anything from the months after Elsie died. I was in bed for weeks, recovering. The war ended in November. We were relieved, but none of us felt much like celebrating.

I didn't even go to Elsie's funeral. Dr. Bender said I was too weak to get out of bed. Afterward, Bertha sat by my bed and told me about the service. None of us could go to Otto's funeral. Health officials had ordered that only immediate families and the priest were allowed to attend burials.

To my right, Joseph was turning cartwheels and chasing birds. In the other direction, Daniel stood with his head bowed before a cluster of graves. The smallest one was carved with an angel. He bent and laid a bouquet of wildflowers on the ground. He walked over to join me, his face somber.

"You sure you don't mind leaving flowers now and then?" he asked, gesturing at the stones.

Both his mother and his sister Molly were buried there.

"Of course not," I said. Daniel pulled me to my feet and kept my hand in his.

"They don't need much. But it's nice to know someone will be visiting them," he said. "They won't feel so alone."

"I won't feel so alone either," I murmured, looking at my sister's headstone.

"What did you say?" Daniel asked, leaning toward me.

"Nothing," I said, pulling my hand free. "You're really leaving then?" I was upset Daniel was leaving, but I wasn't going to let him know. I didn't want him to feel guilty.

Daniel let out a big sigh and nodded. "One of my cousins already lined up a job for me in Oregon. I'll be cutting down trees."

"Sounds dangerous."

"Easier than running a farm by myself," Daniel said with a crooked grin. "And I'll be able to send money to my sisters."

"Have they all moved now?" I asked.

"Lily and Dottie are settled with my aunt in Saint Paul. Betsy has a train ticket to New York tomorrow. Another cousin lined up a job for her at a boarding house."

My heart broke for Daniel. On top of losing his mother and littlest sister, he lost the farm and his remaining family too. And I had abandoned him at the worst time.

"I'm sorry I left that day," I said, my voice hoarse.

"Don't worry about it," Daniel said. "There was nothing anyone could do."

"Do you think you'll ever come back here?"

Daniel shook his head. "What's left for me here?"

I had no answer. Instead, I wrapped my arms around his shoulders and told him goodbye. I was sad. There would no longer be a friend waiting for me on the other side of the forest path.

As I watched Daniel walk away, I thought about loss. I had lost my sister and before that, my mother. Daniel had lost his family and his home. Otto had lost his life before he'd even set foot on a battlefield. My friend Clara did have the flu. She recovered, but her mother didn't. Neither did our classmate Lonnie Sumners. Sometimes I saw Clara here, laying flowers on her mother's grave. Almost everyone I knew had lost someone, either through the war or influenza.

I knew I should count my blessings, and I did. Joseph didn't get sick. I didn't die. The war was over, and the flu had disappeared. I had survived what the papers called the worst plague in four hundred years. It came at a huge cost.

"Oh, Elsie." I sighed, laying my hand on her headstone. "I will never get over this." I would learn to live with the Elsie-size hole in my heart. But I would never stop missing my sister.

Joseph hopped over to me and leaned against me. "I miss her," he said, tracing his fingers over Elsie's name.

"I do too."

He cocked his head. "I like that she's beneath us," he said.

"What?" I asked. "Why?"

"Because she's holding us up," he said simply.

Tears flowed down my face as I bent and hugged him. "You're absolutely right," I said. "The dead are beneath us, holding us up."

I took his hand and we walked home together.

# A NOTE FROM THE AUTHOR

Several years ago, I stood in a long line at a local high school waiting to be vaccinated. It was 2009, and the H1N1 pandemic was spreading across the globe. My older son was a baby at the time, and children under the age of five were at higher risk of developing complications from the flu. This made me very anxious. During the pandemic, I took the same kinds of precautions Daisy and her family took: we avoided most public places, and we washed our hands. But unlike Daisy, we had the option to be vaccinated.

News reports frequently compared the H1N1 pandemic to the 1918 influenza pandemic. I remember wondering about the people who had lived in my old Victorian house during that first pandemic. They had faced the same fears and worries I was now facing but with far fewer resources. In fact, I cringed when I learned that the masks everyone wore in 1918, including Daisy and her family, were pretty useless in preventing infection. My family and I came through the 2009 pandemic just fine, but when I was asked to write a novel about the 1918 influenza pandemic, I jumped at the chance.

Since the pandemic affected the entire world, I first had to settle on the story's setting. I decided to set the novel in a small Minnesota town like mine. This allowed me to explore the major role World War I played in the pandemic. Soldiers like Otto met at training bases and the battlefield. Civilians moved to cities for work. This mobility brought both contact and germs.

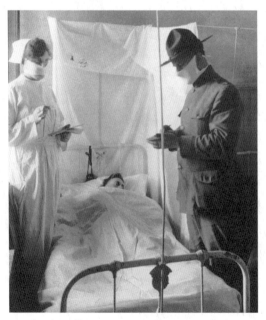

Medical staff at Fort Porter in New York wore masks to protect themselves from influenza.

In the United States, the railroads played a big role in spreading germs, as infected soldiers and the bodies of flu victims were transported across the country. The postman carried germs from house to house too. This is likely how Elsie was infected.

Nurses played an important role caring for the sick during the outbreak. These nurses served as part of the St. Louis Red Cross Motor Corps.

The pandemic ranged from 1918 into 1919, so I also had to decide when during the pandemic to set Daisy's story. The 1918 flu came in three waves. The first reported instances of the flu were in March 1918 at Fort Riley in Kansas. The flu then spread across the United States, Europe, and Asia. It returned with a vengeance in fall 1918. This wave proved to be the deadliest, which is why I ended up setting the story during October 1918. A third wave of influenza came in late winter and spring 1919.

I wanted to get the details correct about how the flu affected the real-life town of New Ulm, Minnesota. While researching influenza in Minnesota, I stumbled on a reference to an unpublished manuscript, *The Influenza Pandemic of 1918: An Overview and Its Effect on Brown County, Concentrating on New Ulm,* written in 2003 by local researcher Darlene Filzen.

I emailed the author and asked if she would be willing to share a copy of the manuscript with me. Not only did she enthusiastically agree, she also included several newspaper clippings from the time period! As a librarian, I like to share this story as a great example of the collaborative nature of research. Many thanks to Darlene for sharing her work with me.

The prejudice Daisy and her family faced as German Americans during World War I was very real. Many New Ulm residents were conflicted by the war, torn between loyalty to their new country and their old. They did not wish to fight relatives and friends overseas. The town held a massive rally to support the draft on July 25, 1917, but several townspeople also spoke out against the war itself.

In the late 1800s and early 1900s, New Ulm was home to many German American residents like Daisy and her family.

The event drew the attention of the Minnesota Public Safety Commission, a group that had been organized by the state to oversee local war efforts. The Commission did not like what they heard. They placed the town of New Ulm under surveillance. Although the group had been formed to keep the state safe during the war, they also targeted anyone accused of being loyal to Germany.

Until I started working on this manuscript, I had no idea that Minnesota, like many states, had formed such a commission. During the war, the Public Safety Commission strongly urged school districts to use English as the primary language. The commission even compiled a list of "questionable" German textbooks that could not be used. Like many German Americans, Daisy would have attended school where German was the primary language of instruction.

Albert Steinhauser, who was the editor of the *New Ulm Review* and the German-language *New Ulm Post*, was charged under the Espionage Act (which was later expanded into the Sedition Act), although he was never prosecuted. The incident Bertha and Daisy discuss about a German American farmer being tarred and feathered is based on a real event. I wanted these instances to remind us of how frighteningly easy it is to mistrust those who do not look or sound like us, and how it leads to no place good.

I still can't wrap my mind around the influenza pandemic's impact. The number of influenza deaths worldwide is staggering. In the United States alone, at least six hundred thousand died. The pandemic killed an estimated fifty million people across the world, although some estimates put the number closer to one hundred million. More people died from influenza than from the war itself.

Native American populations were hit especially hard. The Inupiaq town of Brevig Mission, Alaska, saw 72 of its 80 residents die in less than one week. While Daisy's story is unique, it is also universal. Think of all the people who saw family and friends die from the flu or worried about loved ones not surviving the war. It was a bleak time.

Despite all the loss, I wanted to end the book on a hopeful note. Joseph's words at the end originally came

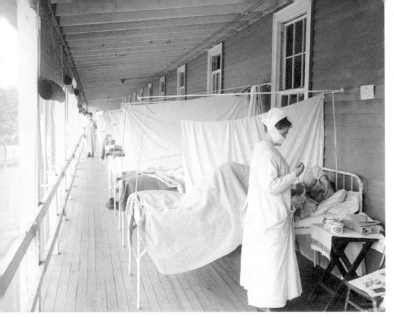

The influenza ward at Walter Reed Hospital in Washington, D.C., was busy during the pandemic. The D.C. area lost nearly 3,000 people to the flu.

from my older son, who talked about the dead holding us up when we visited a cemetery years ago (thanks for letting me use your words, Sam!). Daisy does not shy away from her grief. But she also takes comfort in the love of her family and friends, holiday traditions, and even the fleeting beauty of lilac blossoms. I hope Daisy reminds all of us to cultivate gratitude for the world around us.

# GLOSSARY

**buffet** (buh-FAY)—a piece of furniture with a flat top for serving food and drawers for storing dishes

**carbolic acid** (kahr-BAH-lik AS-ihd)—an organic compound commonly used as a disinfectant

**crepe** (KRAYPE)—a crimped fabric that was traditionally associated with mourning

**draft** (DRAFT)—to make someone join the armed forces

**exile** (EG-zile)—to be sent away or to stay away

**influenza** (in-floo-EN-zuh)—a respiratory illness caused by a highly contagious virus; symptoms include fever, aches, and congestion

**marred** (MAHRD)—wrinkled, spoiled

**marzipan** (MAHR-zih-pan)—a paste made from almond meal and sugar, mainly used in baking

**Model T** (MAH-duhl TEE)—a car built by the Ford Motor Company; one of the first affordable automobiles

**pandemic** (pan-DEM-ik)—a disease affecting a large part of the world

**patriotic** (pay-tree-AH-tik)—loyalty to one's country

**plague** (PLAYG)—a very serious disease that spreads quickly

**rangy** (RAYN-jee)—tall and slender, with long limbs

**Sedition Act** (seh-DISH-uhn AKT)—passed by the United States Congress in 1918 as an extension of the Espionage Act, the Sedition Act forbade speech that appeared to criticize the United States

**stollen** (STOH-luhn)—a traditional German bread stuffed with nuts, spices, and fruit, commonly eaten at Christmas

**tuberculosis** (tuh-bur-kyuh-LOH-sis)—a bacterial infection usually infecting the lungs

# MAKING CONNECTIONS

1. Family relationships play a big role in Daisy's story. At the beginning of the book, Daisy is very close with her sister and brother. She is disappointed in her father and clashes with her stepmother. Which relationship do you think changed the most over the course of the story? Why?

2. Daisy is upset that her father shut down his newspaper because he was scared. She wanted him to take a stand for free speech. What do you think of Emil's decision? Do you think Daisy judged him too harshly, or did Daisy have a point? If you were in Emil's shoes, how do you think you would have reacted?

3. At the end of the novel, Daisy promises her friend Daniel that she will visit his family's graves when she visits Elsie's and her mother's. Do you think she keeps this promise? Why or why not? Do you think Daniel ever returns to New Ulm? Imagine it is five years later. In what ways do you think Daisy continues to remember those who died in the pandemic?

# ABOUT THE AUTHOR

Although Julie Gilbert's masterpiece, *The Adventures of Kitty Bob: Alien Warlord Cat*, has sadly been out of print since she last stapled it together in the fourth grade, Julie continues to write. She is the author of the Dark Waters series from Stone Arch Books. Her novels consider themes of identity and belonging, often with a healthy dose of fantasy and magic. Her short fiction explores topics ranging from airport security lines to adoption to antique wreaths made of hair. She is especially committed to diversity in her writing. Julie makes her home in southern Minnesota with her husband, children, and two lazy cats.

31901068372079